# Karen's Lucky Penny

**Look for these
and other books about Karen
in the
Baby-sitters Little Sister series:**

# BABY-SITTERS
## Little Sister

# Karen's Lucky Penny
## Ann M. Martin

Illustrations by Susan Tang

A
**LITTLE APPLE**
PAPERBACK

SCHOLASTIC INC.
New York Toronto London Auckland Sydney

ISBN 0-590-47048-5

12 11 10 9                                                    0 1 2/0

Printed in the U.S.A.

First Scholastic printing, June 1994

*In honor of the birth of*
*Elizabeth Carpenter Swomley*

# Karen's Lucky Penny

# 1

# The Lucky Penny

"I am hot," said Andrew. "Is it summer yet, Karen?"

"It feels like summer," I replied. "But it is not really summer yet. Not for about three more weeks. We are still having spring."

I am Karen Brewer. I am seven years old. Andrew is my brother. He is four going on five. Andrew and I look alike. We have blond hair and blue eyes. And a few freckles. But I wear glasses and Andrew does not. I even have two pairs of glasses. The blue pair is for reading. The pink pair is for the rest of the time.

Andrew and I live in Stoneybrook, Connecticut. It is a small town. We like Stoneybrook. We were born here. On that hot day at the beginning of June, we were sitting on the curb in front of our mom's house. We were hoping some of our friends would come outside and play. I was especially hoping Nancy Dawes would come outside. Nancy is one of my two best friends. She lives next door with her mom and her dad and her baby brother Danny. Nancy and I have another best friend. Her name is Hannie Papadakis, but she does not live nearby. Hannie and Nancy and I are in the same class, though. We are in Ms. Colman's second grade. We call ourselves the Three Musketeers. We do almost everything together.

"Hi, Karen! Hi, Andrew!"

Someone was running out of the house across the street. It was Kathryn. Her brother Willie was right behind her. (Kathryn is six and Willie is five.)

"Hi!" Andrew and I called back.

Kathryn and Willie crossed the street. They sat on the curb by the sewer with Andrew and me. The four of us sat in a row. Boy, boy, girl, girl. Willie, Andrew, Kathryn, me. We talked about the sewer. We are never sure whether to believe something my big stepbrother Sam once said: that all the sewer pipes in town are connected, and cats walk around in them. They could walk from one end of Stoneybrook to the other without ever seeing the light of day. That is what Sam told me. Honest.

"You know what else?" said Kathryn. (We were still gazing into the sewer.) "I heard that lizards and salamanders get into sewers and they grow huge. Enormous. Like dinosaurs."

"Well, that cannot be true," I replied.

"Why not?" asked Willie.

"Because they would eat the cats. You can't have giant lizards *and* cats walking around the sewers."

"Maybe *Sam's* story is not true," suggested Andrew.

That was very possible.

"Hi, everybody!" Nancy Dawes was running along the sidewalk toward us.

"Nancy!" I cried. "Hi! Come with me to Bobby's house. He left his workbook at school, and Ms. Colman asked me to give it to him."

Bobby Gianelli is in our class, too. He lives down the street. I used to call Bobby a bully, but now we get along (usually). And Bobby's little sister Alicia is Andrew's new friend.

Nancy and I left the other kids behind. We walked to Bobby's house with the workbook.

"I cannot believe school is almost out," said Nancy.

"Me neither," I said. "Then we can have fun, fun, fun in the summertime." (I like school, but I like vacations, too.)

"You know what I want to do?" said Nancy. "I want — "

"Hey!" I cried. "A lucky penny!" On the sidewalk in front of me lay a penny. It was shiny and brand-new. It was also heads-up.

"Ooh, it *is* a lucky penny," said Nancy. "Put it in your pocket, Karen."

I did. I decided to keep it with me at all times.

That penny must have been *really* lucky. When we arrived at Bobby's house, Mrs. Gianelli gave us cookies. Later, I won a game of hopscotch. After dinner, Mr. Tastee, the ice cream man, drove his truck by. And my penny was with me all the time.

# 2

# Two of This and Two of That

Whenever I have good news — and my lucky penny was very good news — I like to share it with my sister Kristy. But guess what. Kristy does not live at my mom's house. That is because she is really my big stepsister. She lives in another part of Stoneybrook with her mom and my dad.

Maybe I better explain something to you. I do not have just one family. I have two. Mommy's family and Daddy's family. And Andrew and I live with both of them. See, long ago, when I was a little kid, I had one family: Mommy, Daddy, Andrew, me. We lived together in a big house. It is the house Daddy grew up in. But Mommy and Daddy began to fight all the time. Finally they said they were going to get a divorce. They did not want to live together anymore. They still loved Andrew and me very much, but they did not love each other. So Mommy moved into a little house, and Daddy stayed in his big house. And Andrew and I began to live at both of their houses. Now we live at Mommy's for a month, then Daddy's for a month. We go back and forth. (We are spending June at the little house.)

Guess what. Mommy and Daddy have gotten married again, but not to each other. Mommy married a man named Seth Engle. He is our stepfather. Daddy married a woman named Elizabeth Thomas. She is our stepmother. And that is how Andrew and I wound up with two families.

This is my little-house family: Mommy, Seth, Andrew, me, Rocky, Midgie, Emily Junior, and Bob. Rocky and Midgie are

Seth's cat and dog. Emily Junior is my pet rat. Bob is Andrew's hermit crab.

This is my big-house family: Daddy, Elizabeth, Kristy, Sam, Charlie, David Michael, Emily Michelle, Nannie, Andrew, me, Boo-Boo, Shannon, Goldfishie, Crystal Light the Second, Emily Junior, and Bob. (Isn't it a good thing that Daddy's house is big?) Kristy, Sam, Charlie, and David Michael are Elizabeth's kids. (She was married once before she married Daddy.) Kristy is thirteen and I love her. She is one of my favorite people. (That is why I wanted to tell her about my lucky penny.) Sam and Charlie are old. They go to high school. David Michael is seven like me, but we go to different schools. Emily Michelle is my adopted sister. She is two and a half. Daddy and Elizabeth adopted her from the faraway country of Vietnam. Nannie is Elizabeth's mother. That makes her my stepgrandmother. She helps take care of all the people and pets at the big house. And these are the pets: Boo-Boo is Daddy's scratchy old cat, Shannon is David Michael's big puppy, Crystal Light and Goldfishie are goldfish (duh), and you know who Emily Junior and Bob are. (They go back and forth with Andrew and me.)

I made up special names for my brother and me. I call us Andrew Two-Two and Karen Two-Two. (I got the idea for those names after Ms. Colman read a book to our class. It was called *Jacob Two-Two Meets the Hooded Fang*.) I decided we are two-twos because we have two of so many things. We have two houses and two families, two mommies and two daddies, two cats and two dogs. I have two stuffed cats that look just the same. Moosie stays at the big house and Goosie stays at the little house. Plus I have two bicycles, one at each house. (Andrew has two tricycles.) And we have toys and books and clothes at each house. (This is so we do not have to pack much when we go back and forth.) And of course I have those two pairs of glasses. I even have my two best friends. Nancy lives next door to

Mommy, and Hannie lives across the street from Daddy and one house down.

Being a two-two is not always easy. For instance, sometimes Andrew and I forget things at one house or the other. Plus, when we are at the little house, we miss our big-house family. And when we are at the big house, we miss our little-house family. But becoming two-twos was the best way to work things out. Usually, I am glad I am a two-two. In fact, sometimes I feel lucky. As lucky as my lucky penny.

3

# T. Rex

One day after school, Bobby and Alicia and Kathryn and Willie and Hannie and Nancy and Andrew and I were playing outside. (Hannie had ridden home with Nancy and me after school.) Kathryn was trying to teach Alicia to jump rope. Andrew was trying out Willie's two-wheeler, which had training wheels. And Bobby and my friends and I were sitting in the grass and talking.

"You know what I really want to do this summer?" Nancy asked.

I could not think of anything better than going to circus camp, which is what Hannie and Nancy and I were going to do in July. So I said, "What?"

"I want to go to Funland."

"That would be so, so cool!" agreed Hannie.

Funland is an amusement park. It is brand-new. It just opened. My friends and I have seen lots of ads for it on TV.

"Who's going to Funland?" asked Andrew. He was wobbling by us on Willie's bike. If he had ridden any slower, he would have been standing still.

"No one," I replied.

"But we all want to," added Bobby.

"Could we really go?" asked Alicia.

Bobby shrugged.

"Is it very far away?" asked Kathryn.

Nancy and I looked at each other. "It is probably about an hour away," I said. Nancy nodded.

"I want to play games and win prizes!" said Hannie.

"I want to go on the water rides," said Willie.

"I want to go on the Ferris wheel," said Andrew.

"I *really* want to go on T. Rex," I said.

Everyone wanted to go on T. Rex. The TV commercials for Funland kept showing people on the park's best ride, T. Rex. It was supposed to be a wild trip through dinosaur land. People wanted to go on that ride so badly that sometimes they waited on line for two hours. That is what Chris in my class had said. And he should know. He had already been to Funland and ridden on T. Rex — twice. He told us about it during Show and Share.

"Well, *could* we go to Funland?" asked Alicia again.

"All of us?" I replied. "Maybe. Hmm . . ."

"Wouldn't it be fun to go together?" said Nancy, sounding excited. "We could go after school lets out. All of our families. One big group."

Hannie looked disappointed. "*My* family

will not be able to go," she said. "Not this summer. Because of Daddy's work schedule and Linny's camp."

"Maybe you could come with my family," I said.

"Let's talk to our parents. Tonight," added Bobby.

So we did. At suppertime I held onto my lucky penny in my pocket. I rubbed it between my fingers. "Mommy? Seth?" I said. "Could we go to Funland this summer? With the Gianellis and Nancy's family and Kathryn's family? And could we bring Hannie with us?" I told them what my friends and I had been talking about that afternoon.

Mommy and Seth did not say no and they did not say yes. They did say, "Do you know what the admission charge for Funland is?"

"No," said Andrew and I.

"It is forty dollars for adults and twenty-five dollars for kids under twelve."

"*Forty dollars?*" I repeated. "Oh, no. We will never get to go!"

"Well, let us think about it," said Mommy.

"Really?"

"Really."

When Andrew and I went outside again after dinner, our friends were there. Guess what. Their parents had said they would think about the trip, too. This was a good sign. I rubbed my penny for luck.

# Andrew's Jobs

"Mommy?" said Andrew. "I need a job."

It was after-school snacktime. Mommy and Andrew and I were sitting at the kitchen table. We were eating grapes.

"What do you need a job for?" I asked. "Do you want to get your own apartment?"

Andrew giggled. "No. I just need money."

That was probably true. Andrew gets a teeny, tiny allowance since he is still just four. Mostly, he is broke all the time.

"But what do you need money for?" I asked him.

"Oh . . . things."

"Okay," said Mommy. "Let me think."

I took my brother into the rec room. "Andrew," I said, "you have to go about this in the right way." (Andrew is too little for most jobs. He does some chores at the big house and the little house. But no one would hire him to walk a dog or mow a lawn. Still, he could earn some money.) "You have to be grown-up and sensible about this," I told him.

"Okay."

"What you should do is tell Mommy you will do lots of chores around the house. Like, you could dust the living room for twenty-five cents. Or empty the wastebaskets for ten cents. Or sweep the front walk, or carry the laundry downstairs. You can do lots of things. You are already good at dusting and at making your bed. I will help you figure out how much to charge."

Andrew told Mommy he was ready to work around the house.

His first job was dusting the living room. Mommy paid him *fifty* cents. (I decided Andrew did not need my help anymore.) Next he swept off the walk. Then he took the garbage out. And he kept on going. Each time Andrew finished a job, I heard *clink*, *clink* as he dropped coins into his china bank. His bank was starting to fill up.

I decided I better count the money in my own bank. I opened it up and dumped out the coins. I had exactly three dollars and sixty-two cents. Then I remembered my lucky penny. That made three sixty-three. (Even though I would never spend that penny.) Three sixty-three. That was not a lot of money. But I could not think of anything I needed to buy.

At dinner that night, I said to Mommy

and Seth, "Have you decided about the trip to Funland yet?" That was a silly question. They would have said something if they had. Sure enough, they had not made up their minds yet. I decided not to bug them anymore.

# Funland

Two days later, Mommy and Seth and Andrew and I were having corn-on-the-cob for dinner. Since the weather was so warm, we were eating at the picnic table in the yard. Andrew was making such a mess that Seth had tucked Andrew's napkin into the collar of his shirt. "You are a butterball," Seth said.

When Andrew was all taken care of, Mommy said, "Well, Seth and I have talked to the other parents, and we have made a decision about Funland."

"You have?" I glanced across the table at Andrew.

"Yes," replied Mommy. She began to smile. "Sometime after school has let out, and before circus camp begins, we will take a group trip to Funland."

"And your mom and I will be happy to bring Hannie along," added Seth.

"Yes!" Andrew and I cried. "Oh, thank you, thank you, thank you!"

"There is just one thing," Mommy went on. "The grown-ups will pay the admission fees and buy lunch. But you kids must bring along your own money for snacks and souvenirs and playing midway games."

That sounded fair to me. "Okay," I said.

"Okay," said Andrew.

After dinner that night, Andrew and I met up with our friends. We all knew the news by then, and we were very excited. We stood around on the lawn in front of the little house.

"I cannot wait to ride T. Rex!" exclaimed Bobby.

"I am going to win a big pink teddy bear," announced Kathryn.

"I want to ride the Ferris wheel," said Andrew. "But I hope I do not get stuck at the top. That is too scary."

"Hannie loves getting stuck at the top of — " I started to say. And then I cried, "Oh, my gosh! Hannie! I forgot to tell her that she can come to Funland with us."

Nancy and I ran inside. We called Hannie. "Guess what!" I said to her. "We are going to Funland! All of us. My family and Nancy's and everyone. And you can come with us. You are invited!"

Hannie shrieked so loudly I had to hold the phone away from my ear. Then I shrieked. Then Nancy shrieked. Then Seth called from the living room, "Indoor voices, girls!"

Nancy and I said good-bye to Hannie and ran outside again.

"You know what?" I said to my friends. "I think this happened because of my lucky penny." I kissed the penny, then stuck it in my pocket.

"Speaking of money," said Bobby, "we are going to need a lot. Souvenirs and games can be expensive. I bet I only have two or three dollars."

"Same here," said Kathryn and Nancy.

"Me too," I said. "Three sixty-two, not counting my penny."

"I only have one dollar," said Willie.

Alicia did not have any money.

I looked at Andrew. "How much did you earn?" I asked him.

"I have eight quarters and nine dimes. I just counted them."

Eight quarters and nine dimes? That was —

"Two dollars and ninety cents!" said Nancy. "Wow. That is pretty much."

And it was. For a little kid.

"Thanks," replied Andrew. Then he added, "I will be earning even more. I can do lots of chores for Mommy and Seth."

I smiled sadly at my brother. Poor kid. He had no idea. How much money could he *really* earn dusting something for fifty cents, sweeping something for a quarter? I decided I would be a nice big sister and lend him money at Funland if he needed it. Which he probably would.

"Boy," said Bobby a few minutes later. "We better figure out how to earn money for the trip. I will need more than two dollars."

"And we don't have much time," added Nancy. "Just a few weeks."

We sat down on the curb to think.

# 6

# The Lost Wallet

The next day, Nancy came over after school. We were roller skating up and down the sidewalk when Bobby came by. "Hi" he called.

"Hi, Bobby!" said Nancy and I.

"Want to go to the brook with me?" he asked.

There is a little brook not far from Bobby's house. I had almost forgotten about it. It is pretty boring in the wintertime. But now that summer was almost here, that brook would be full of minnows. And we would probably see dragonflies and water spiders and newts and maybe frogs.

"Yes!" I exclaimed. "Okay, Nancy?"

"Okay."

Nancy and I took off our skates. We put on our shoes. Then we followed Bobby down the street. My hand was in my pocket, and I rubbed the lucky penny. I was thinking about earning money.

So were Nancy and Bobby. "We should start a business," Nancy was saying.

I was not looking at her. My eyes were on the ground. I was hoping to find another lucky penny. I would give it to Andrew.

I found something else instead.

It was brown and leathery, and it was sticking out from under a bush that grew close to the sidewalk.

"Hey, you guys! Wait a second," I said. I stopped. I reached under the bush. And I pulled out a wallet.

The wallet was very fat.

"Whoa," said Nancy as she peered over my shoulder.

I stuck my hand in my pocket and gave the penny one more rub for good luck. Then I opened the wallet. It was *stuffed* with money.

I thought Bobby was going to have a heart attack. "Count it! Count it! Count it!" he cried, jumping up and down.

Slowly and carefully, Nancy and I counted the bills. This took a long time. When we finally finished, we just stared at each other.

"Almost eight hundred dollars," I whispered. "A fortune."

"I wonder who it belongs to," said Nancy.

We checked everything in the wallet. We could not find a name or an address anywhere. Just a couple of kids' school pictures and a little calendar.

Bobby whistled. "It's yours then. The money is all yours."

"It *is*?" I could not believe that.

"Sure. Finders keepers. How would you know who to return the wallet to?"

"Well . . . I don't know." I looked at the photos again. On the back of one was written "To Daddy." On the back of the other was written "For Dad." But no names. "I just — " I started to say.

"Karen, think what you could buy with all that money," said Bobby.

"Think what you could do at Funland," added Nancy.

"Are you *sure* it's okay to keep this?" I asked.

"Sure I'm sure," replied Bobby. "It is almost a rule: If you do not see a name, then finders keepers." Bobby sounded awfully sure of himself.

And I wanted to spend eight hundred dollars at Funland. I could buy every souvenir I saw. I could eat all the cotton candy I wanted. I could play the midway games until I won ten teddy bears.

"Okay, then. I guess the money is mine," I said.

"You could split it with Nancy and me," suggested Bobby. "Since we were with you when you found the wallet."

"Oh, no. I found it all by myself," I replied. But I felt a little greedy. So I opened the wallet and took out two five-dollar bills. I gave one to Bobby and one to Nancy.

"Thanks!" they said.

Then I stuffed the wallet into my pocket. I began to walk home. I decided not to go to the brook. I did not think I should go wading around with eight hundred dollars. That did not seem safe. Besides, I needed to think. I had already decided not to tell Mommy and Seth about finding the wallet. But what would I tell them when they asked how I had gotten so rich?

# 7

# Jail

I had found the wallet on Thursday afternoon. I had hidden it in my room. I had not told anyone I had found it. I made Nancy and Bobby promise not to tell anyone either. The trouble was that now I could not spend it. If I bought anything big, Mommy and Seth would want to know where I got the money for it. They thought I had only a few dollars.

By Friday, I began to feel funny about the hidden wallet. Was it *really* okay to keep it? If it was, then why was I hiding it? I did not think keeping the wallet was exactly wrong. But I did not think it was quite right either. On the other hand, I wanted to be able to spend that money at Funland. One of the Funland TV commercials showed a girl wearing a Funland visor, T-shirt, sunglasses, socks, belt bag, and backpack, and carrying a Funland teddy bear, drinking cup, pennant, bank, doll, sleeping bag, and so many other things she could hardly move. I wanted to look just like that girl. And when I thought about it, I wanted a few other things that I would be able to buy now that I had eight hundred dollars.

I looked at the spot where I had hidden the wallet. The wallet was stuffed behind some books on my shelf. Then I thought, what would happen if Mommy and Seth found the wallet all hidden away in my room? Maybe they would think I had stolen it. And if they did maybe I would have to go to *jail*. Jail. How could I go to jail when I also had to go to second grade? What would Mommy say to Ms. Colman? "I am sorry, Ms. Colman, but Karen cannot come to school today because she is in the pokey."

I sighed. I took the wallet out of its hiding place. I stared at it for a few moments. Then I opened it. I counted the money again. I thought about Funland. Then I thought about being behind bars.

On Friday night I did not sleep well. I kept waking up, and imagining myself in one of those striped jail outfits.

By Saturday morning I had made a decision. I knew what I had to do. I took the wallet out of its new hiding place. (I had been moving the wallet around my room because I was never sure the hiding places were good enough. I kept changing them.)

Then I carried it through the hallway.

I started down the stairs. "Mommy! Seth!" I called. "Can I talk to you? I have to tell you something important."

# The Police

Mommy and Seth and I sat at the kitchen table. The wallet lay on the table in front of me. For a moment, Mommy and Seth just stared at it.

Finally Seth said, "Imagine carrying around all that cash with no identification." He shook his head.

"Where did you say you found it?" Mommy asked me.

"Kind of under a bush, right by the sidewalk. We were near Bobby's house."

"And this was on Thursday?" said Seth.

I nodded. "Yes. And Bobby said I could keep the money. He said that was okay, since we do not know who the wallet belongs to." I could tell that Mommy and Seth were about to say something like, "But, Karen, don't you think whoever lost this wallet will want all his money?" So before that could happen I said quickly, "If I did anything wrong, I am really, really sorry. Really. Bobby *said* it was okay. But now I am not sure he was right. Anyway, all of the money is still in the wallet. Except for ten dollars. I gave five dollars each to Nancy and Bobby. I did not want them to feel bad because I had so much money and they were broke."

"Well," said Mommy, "I guess you know what we have to do now, Karen."

"Try to find the owner," I replied. "But how are we going to do that?"

"We will take the wallet to the police. They will know what to do."

"Right," agreed Seth. "Someone may already have asked the police if anyone turned in a lost wallet. And that person could identify the wallet by saying how much money was in it, and describing the wallet and the school pictures."

"And," said Mommy, "if the owner does show up, he will want *all* of his money. You were nice to give some to your friends, Karen, but we have to replace it." Mommy took ten dollars out of her own purse and put it in the wallet.

Then we drove to the police station. Andrew came with us. He says he likes police stations. He thinks the police live there. (He also thinks his teacher lives in her classroom.)

At the police station, Mommy told my story to an officer. Then I handed over the wallet. The officer looked inside it. She counted the money.

"My," she said. "You would think someone would have called to ask about the wallet. This is an awful lot of money."

"Maybe the person does not know where

he lost it," suggested Seth. "He might not even live in Stoneybrook."

"Do you mean that no one has called to say he lost a wallet?" I asked the officer hopefully. (I rubbed my lucky penny.)

"Not that I know of, but I better check," she replied. "I just came on duty. Someone might have called last night."

The officer disappeared. When she came back she was shaking her head. "No one called. None of the officers knows anything about a missing wallet or missing money. When did you find this?"

"On Thursday."

I was about to apologize again for keeping it, but the officer was scratching her head. She was not looking at me. "Thursday," she repeated. "And we do not know how long the wallet had been lying under the bush before you found it. Hmm. Well, let's say the wallet has been lost for three days already. That's a long time. But as you said, Mr. Engle, the owner may not know where he lost it, so he may not know which police station to call. We should give him some more time to claim the wallet."

"What if he does not claim it?" I asked. "How long do we wait?"

The officer thought for a moment. Then she gave me a date.

"That does not sound too bad," I said.

"I will keep you posted. And feel free to call me whenever you want. Just ask for Officer Benitez. That's me."

"Okay. Thanks!" I rubbed the lucky penny and crossed all my fingers.

9

# Money Trouble

When we arrived home from the police station, the kids were playing outside as usual — Kathryn and Willie, Bobby and Alicia and Nancy. Andrew and I jumped out of the car and ran to them. Andrew ran straight to Alicia. He calls Alicia his best friend now. I ran to Nancy and Bobby. They were standing apart from the other kids. They were talking about something. And they looked very serious. At first they did not even see me.

"Hi! Hi, Nancy! Hi, Bobby!" I said.

"Oh, hi, Karen."

"What are you guys doing?"

"We are still thinking of ways to earn money."

"Goody, let me help you. I love thinking up plans."

Nancy gave me a funny look. "Why do *you* need to plan ways to earn money?" she asked me. "You have plenty of money."

I shook my head. "Not anymore."

"What happened?" exclaimed Bobby. "Where is the money?"

"At the police station. Mommy and Seth made me give the wallet back. I just could not keep it a secret. When I told them about it, they said we had to go to the police. They said whoever lost all that money would want it back badly."

"What did the police say?" asked Nancy.

"They said no one has called about a lost wallet yet. But they are going to hold onto the wallet for awhile. If the owner calls, they will give him the wallet. If no one calls, then I get to keep the money."

"So you still might be loaded," said Bobby.

"And I might not be. Right now I have hardly any money for Funland. Oh, and by the way, you guys each owe Mommy five dollars. She said if I was going to give the wallet back, all the money should be in it. So she put back the ten dollars I gave you. She took it out of her wallet."

Nancy's mouth dropped open.

Bobby cried, "But that isn't fair! You *gave* us that money."

"Plus, I already spent my five dollars," said Nancy. "I meant to save it for Funland but, well, I didn't."

"Same here," said Bobby. "Nancy and I are both almost broke. That is why we have to think up a business to go into. We have to earn a lot of money fast."

"If you are going to earn a lot of money, then you can pay back Mommy," I said.

"But Karen, you did not tell us we would have to give back the money," said Nancy.

"I did not know I would have to give back the wallet," I replied.

"Anyway, we are probably not going to earn a *lot* of money," said Bobby. "Just enough for Funland."

I looked at Bobby and Nancy. They stared back at me. We did not know how to solve our problem. But I really thought my friends should fork over the ten dollars.

I left Bobby and Nancy. I needed to earn money, but I had a feeling they did not want to plan businesses with me just then. I decided to see what the other kids were doing. Guess what. They were talking about money, too.

"My birthday is next week," said Willie. "I am going to save my birthday money for Funland. I bet I will have a lot."

"Lucky duck," said Alicia.

"I am going to earn money watering Mr. Drucker's plants," said Kathryn.

"I do not know how I will earn money," said Alicia.

"I have already earned money doing

chores for Mommy," said Andrew. "But I need to earn more. I am thinking of having a lemonade stand."

"A lemonade stand?" I repeated.

"Yes," replied Andrew.

"Do you know how to run one?" I asked him.

"You — you just pour the lemonade in the cups and when someone says he wants to buy some you say, 'That will be twenty-five cents, please.' Don't you?"

"Well, not exactly," I said. "Listen, Andrew, be sure to let me help you if you start a lemonade stand."

## 10

# Mr. Beadle

I was counting off the days I had to wait until the wallet might be mine. Only two were left. Nobody had called the police station. I imagined myself taking all that money home. Seven years old — with eight hundred dollars to spend. Well, Mommy and Seth would probably make me put some of it in the bank. But even if I put half in the bank I would still have four hundred. I tried to figure out how many Funland souvenirs I could buy with four hundred dollars.

That afternoon the phone rang. Mommy answered it. She spoke to the caller for a minute or two. Then she hung up. "Karen!" she called. "Can you come to the kitchen, please? I need to talk to you."

I wondered if I was in trouble. What had I done? I could not think of a thing. "Yes?" I said when I reached Mommy.

"Honey, someone claimed the wallet a little while ago. The police are sure he is the owner. He described the school pictures and the wallet and everything."

"Darn!" I cried. I stamped my foot. "I don't believe it. That money was mine."

"Karen," said Mommy. "No, it was not. It belongs to Mr. Beadle. He is the owner. And he worked very hard to earn it."

"I guess," I replied.

"Also, he would like to meet you," Mommy went on.

"He would?"

"Yes. And he is at the police station right now."

Mommy and Andrew and I piled into the

car and drove to the station. Officer Benitez met us there. "Come say hi to Mr. Beadle, Karen," she said. "He wants to meet the person who was honest enough to turn in his wallet."

We went into a small room. A man was sitting at a table. He looked like he might be just a little older than Daddy. And he was dressed in very plain clothes — a worn-out shirt and faded jeans. He grinned when I walked into the room.

"Mr. Beadle, this is Karen Brewer," said Officer Benitez.

Mr. Beadle jumped to his feet. "Karen," he said, "I cannot tell you how relieved I am that you turned in my wallet. Not everyone would have been as honest as you were. That money means a lot to my family and me. Thank you so much."

"You're welcome," I replied.

"I'd — I'd like to give you a reward, Karen," Mr. Beadle went on.

I almost said, "Really? How much?" Instead I said, "Oh. Thank you."

At the very same time, Mommy said, "We cannot take any money."

"But I insist," said Mr. Beadle. "A reward is in order."

I looked at Mommy. I looked at Mr. Beadle. Maybe Mr. Beadle would split his money with me. Four hundred dollars for each of us.

Mr. Beadle was reaching into the wallet. He pulled out some bills and counted them. Then he placed them in my hand. "There you go, Karen," he said. "One hundred dollars. And thank you again."

"One hundred dollars!" I cried. One hundred? What had happened to four hundred?

"One hundred dollars!" Mommy cried. "Oh, no. That is far too much!"

"Once again, I insist," said Mr. Beadle. And with that he stood up and walked out of the room. The rest of us followed him.

"*Thank* him," Mommy whispered to me.

"Thank you, Mr. Beadle," I said. Then I added, "Thank you very much."

"My goodness," Mommy said a few moments later as we climbed into our car. "One hundred dollars, Karen. That is a lot of money."

"I know. It isn't as much as eight hundred, though. Mommy? Could I keep all the money? I mean, do I have to put some of it in the bank? Just this once, couldn't I keep it all? Please?"

"Oh, honey, I don't know. What are you going to do with it?"

"Spend it, I guess. On Funland and maybe some other things."

"That might be harder than it sounds," said Mommy. (I did not see how. I love to spend money.) "But all right. This one time you do not have to put anything in the bank. I just hope you learn something from spending the money, Karen. Spend it wisely."

# 11

## Toys

I could not believe my good luck. Okay, so Mr. Beadle had shown up and I had not been able to keep the eight hundred dollars. I did not even have four hundred dollars. But I had one hundred dollars. And Mommy had said I could do whatever I wanted with it. I was all set for Funland. I could buy plenty of souvenirs.

When Mommy and Andrew and I arrived home from the police station, Andrew and I ran outside to play. I was still holding my reward money. I waved the bills around.

"Guess what I have here!" I cried.

Bobby and Nancy stopped talking and looked at me.

Alicia and Kathryn and Willie stopped making their chalk drawings and looked at me.

"She has a hun — " Andrew started to say.

"No!" I cried. "Let me tell. I have a hundred dollars! And it is all mine to spend. The guy who lost the wallet called the police. They gave the wallet back to him, but he gave me one hundred dollars for a reward."

"Cool," said Nancy.

"Yeah," agreed Bobby. "Now you can pay your mom back for us. You will still have ninety dollars for Funland."

I frowned. "But *you* owe my mom the money. You and Nancy. I gave it to *you*."

"Right," said Bobby. "You *gave* it to us. We did not ask for it. And you did not say you were going to want it back."

But I had not *known* I would want it back.

"I will have to think about it," I told my friends.

"Karen? Are you going to spend *all* your money at Funland?" Kathryn wanted to know. "All one hundred dollars?"

"All ninety dollars," muttered Bobby, but I ignored him.

"Well . . ." Hmm. That was a good question. I did not need *that* much money for Funland. Maybe I did not *really* need to look like the girl in the TV commercial. I could spend half of my money on other things, and still have plenty for our trip. "No," I told Kathryn. "It is not all for Funland."

"What else are you going to buy?" asked Willie.

"I do not know yet," I replied. "I have to think about it." I looked down at my fistful of money. "Right now, I better go put this someplace safe." If I was going to show Mommy that I could spend my money wisely, I better not start off by losing it.

I ran inside to my bedroom. I found my

bank and stuffed the bills into it. Then I sat down to think about how I could spend the money. On a pad of paper I wrote: *Funland*. I lifted my pencil. I could not think what to write next. Then I remembered some toys and things I wanted. I listed:

BUBBLE BLASTER
PINK SLIPPERS WITH WHITE FUZZY TRIM FOR
  DRESS-UP
NEW MARKERS
GLOW-IN-THE-DARK BUGS
SOMETHING FOR ANDREW
STICKERS
ART SUPPLIES

I thought that was a pretty wise list. All the things I wrote down were things I really wanted. And they were not too expensive. Plus, I had remembered to include Andrew. Mommy would like that.

I stood up. Then I leaned against my window and looked outside. I could hear Bobby and Nancy talking.

Bobby was saying, "We could rake leaves."

Nancy replied, "What leaves? It's still spring. The leaves won't fall for months. Not until autumn."

"Oh, yeah," said Bobby.

He looked a little sad. I guess he and Nancy had not decided on a business to go into yet.

That gave me an idea. I decided to do some nice things for my friends, just like I was going to buy a toy for Andrew. Now what could I do for them? I sat down to think.

# 12

# The Movies

School was almost over. Only a few more days were left, and they were half days. I was a little sad about the end of school. But not too sad. After school ended, I could look forward to Funland.

I had had my one hundred dollars for two whole days and I had not spent a penny of it. Instead I had been watching my friends scramble around, trying to earn their own money. In school, Nancy and Hannie sat on the desks in the back of the room and talked. (Bobby would not talk to us girls during school, only after school.)

I joined my friends. "I have been thinking," I said. "The Three Musketeers need a treat. Let's go to a movie. We can go in the afternoon since we only have school in the morning now."

"Karen. We do not have any money," said Hannie.

"I know. My treat. I really want to take you. And I will pay for everything. We can ask Kristy to come with us."

And that is just what we did. On Monday afternoon, my big stepbrother Charlie dropped us off at the movie theater — Kristy, Hannie, Nancy, and me.

"This is so cool, Karen!" exclaimed Hannie. "Thank you!"

"Double thank you," added Nancy. "Don't you feel grown-up?"

I did. I felt especially grown-up when I stepped up to the ticket window and said,

"Three, please." (Kristy had said she would buy her own ticket.) Then I handed the man some money.

"Treating your friends?" he asked me.

I nodded proudly. "Yup."

We walked inside. There, right in front of us, was the refreshment counter. Popcorn, candy, ice cream, and sodas.

"What do you guys want?" I asked Hannie and Nancy. "I will buy you whatever you want." Then I added, "Within reason." That is what Mommy and Seth always say. It means don't go overboard.

"Popcorn," said Nancy.

"Popcorn," said Hannie.

"And sodas, please?" added Nancy.

In the end, I bought one enormous tub of popcorn for the four of us to share, plus three sodas. (Kristy bought her own soda.) Then we carried our things to the ticket taker. Kristy handed him hers. I handed him the three for my friends and me. The man ripped them in half, then gave us back one half each. I grinned at my friends. We hardly ever get to go to the movies unless we are with someone's parents.

Kristy led us into the dark theater. "Where do you guys want to sit?" she asked. (The theater was practically empty.)

"In the front," I said.

"In the back," said Nancy.

"I don't care," said Hannie.

We settled on the middle.

"Kristy? Could you sit *behind* us?" I asked. "Then we would feel like we had really come to the movies by ourselves."

Kristy sat behind us. My friends and I passed the popcorn back and forth. (We remembered to pass it to Kristy, too.) Soon the lights were turned out. A cartoon began. Then the feature came on. We had decided to see *The Tale of the Bad Dog*, which sounded funny.

When the movie ended, Hannie grinned at me. "That was great, Karen!"

And Nancy added, "I just love feeling

grown-up. Thank you again for treating us.
I am glad we are the Three Musketeers."

Then Kristy whispered to me from behind, "You are a good friend, Karen."

I was glad I could share my money.

# 13

# Mr. Tastee

One evening my friends and I were playing statues in Kathryn and Willie's front yard. The air was warm. Summer had finally arrived. School was out.

"You moved! I saw you move!" Kathryn called to Alicia.

"Did not!" Alicia replied.

"I did too see you!"

"But I did not move!"

"But I — "

Andrew stepped in. "She did not move."

"Thank you, Andrew," said Alicia.

Nancy cupped her hand around my ear. "I think Andrew likes Alicia."

"He calls her his best friend," I said.

"I think she is his girlfriend."

I giggled. But I stopped suddenly. "Hey! Nancy, do you hear that?"

"Hear what?"

"Listen. Bells. Mr. Tastee is coming!"

Mr. Tastee, the ice cream man, cruises his truck slowly through the streets of our neighborhood in the summertime. When we run to the street he stops for us. Then we can buy Popsicles and ice-cream cones and ice-cream sandwiches. They have funny names. The Spaceship, Triple Trouble, Goofy Nuts, Bitty Buddy. Do you know what I once found out? The man who drives the truck is not *really* named Mr. Tastee. His true name is Roger Jones. But I still like his ice cream. And I still call him Mr. Tastee.

"Come on! We have to get our money!" I cried to my friends. We are always afraid that if we are not fast enough — if we stay in our houses too long looking for change — Mr. Tastee will drive right by us.

But when I started to run across the street, nobody ran after me. The kids stayed in the yard. "Don't you want ice cream?" I asked them.

"We are saving our money," Bobby replied.

I stopped running. "Oh." Hmm. I could not buy ice cream all by myself. That would not be any fun. Also, it would not be fair. I thought for a moment. I still had not bought any toys or any of the things on my list. The only money I had spent was on the movie tickets and our refreshments.

So I ran into my house anyway. I ran straight upstairs to my bank and pulled out a few dollars. Then I dashed outside. I was just in time. Mr. Tastee was coming down the street.

"Stop! Stop!" I cried, waving the money in the air.

Mr. Tastee pulled over to the curb. "Hi, Karen. Are you the only one buying ice cream?" he asked. He was looking at my friends. They were sitting sadly in a row on the curb on the other side of the street.

"I am the only one buying ice cream, but I will not be the only one eating it," I replied. "Tonight I am going to treat my friends."

Mr. Tastee smiled. "Come here, kids," he said. "Ice cream for everyone tonight."

My friends jumped to their feet.

"Really?" cried Nancy.

"You mean it?" said Bobby.

"Of course," I replied.

So we stood at the back of the ice cream truck. We looked at the pictures of the things we could buy. Sometimes we have trouble making up our minds.

Andrew had the most trouble. After all the other kids had chosen, and while they were licking and slurping away, Andrew still stood by the truck.

"Can I really get *any*thing I want, Karen?"

Andrew probably wanted the Chocolate

Dream, which is the most expensive Popsicle. "You can really get anything you want," I told him.

"Okay," said Andrew. "I would like vanilla ice cream, please."

So that is what Mr. Tastee gave him.

Then my friends and my brother thanked me, and I felt very happy.

## 14

# Andrew's Lemonade Stand

A few more days went by. I did not spend any of my money. Also, Andrew did not mention his lemonade stand. I thought he had forgotten about it.

But he had not.

One morning, right after breakfast, he said, "Well, today I am going to have my lemonade stand. I will earn big bucks."

I had my doubts. What did Andrew know about running a lemonade stand? I looked at Mommy, but she did not say anything. So I said, "I better help you, Andrew."

"Why?" he asked.

"Well . . . okay, what is the first thing you do?"

"Put the lemonade outside," he replied.

"What lemonade? We do not have any. Look in the refrigerator."

Andrew looked. No lemonade. "Oh, we have to *make* it first," he said.

"Right. *If* we have any lemonade mix."

Luckily, we did. (Andrew looked relieved.) We made two pitchers and left them in the refrigerator.

"Now you have to set up your stand," I told my brother. "What do you want to use? How about the picnic table?"

"Okay."

Andrew and I lugged the picnic table across the lawn to the sidewalk.

"Now what are you going to pour the lemonade into?" I asked.

"Gl — " I could tell that Andrew had been about to say "glasses." But he had

70

realized that Mommy would never let him take real glasses outside. "Paper cups?" he said instead.

"Good idea." (We found a stack of paper cups.)

"Is my stand ready yet?" asked Andrew.

"Not exactly. How much are you going to charge for the lemonade?"

"Um, twenty-five cents for each cup?"

"Okay. What if your first customer gives you a dollar bill?"

Andrew had not thought about making change. It turned out he had not thought about advertising, either. I had to do everything for him. But at last his stand was ready. Andrew stood behind it, with his cups and lemonade and a box of change.

"Where are my customers?" he asked.

We looked up and down the street. It was empty. "You might have to wait awhile," I told my brother.

"But I do not want to wait. I want to earn money!"

I had an idea. "Okay, you stay here with your stand. I will be back."

I ran next door to Nancy's house. "Nancy," I said, when she had answered the bell, "would you please go buy some lemonade from Andrew?"

Nancy shook her head. "I can't. I am saving my money."

"Oh." I felt in my pockets. I had some change. I pulled out a quarter and gave it to Nancy. "Here," I said. "My treat."

Then I went to Bobby and Alicia's house, and to Kathryn and Willie's house. On the street, I ran into a couple of other kids. I gave every one of them a quarter to buy lemonade from Andrew.

By the time I returned to the stand, my brother's change box was filling up.

"Karen! Look! I am rich!" cried Andrew.

Kathryn was sitting on the lawn. She was still finishing her lemonade. "Yum. That was delicious. Thank you, Karen."

"Yeah, thanks, Karen!" called a few other

kids who were leaving. "Thanks for the quarters!"

Andrew looked at me. He narrowed his eyes. "Karen, you gave them money?"

"Well, yes," I admitted.

"You thought no one would come to my stand, right? You thought I could not do this by myself. You think I am just a baby."

"I'm sorry, Andrew," I said. I did not know what else to say.

# 15

# Karen's Shopping Spree

I left Andrew and his stand outside. I went to my room for awhile. Why was my brother so upset with me? I had only wanted to help him. I lay down on my bed. I thought about what I had done. I had seen that no one was going to come to Andrew's stand, and I did not want him to be disappointed. So I helped him out. I found customers for him. And he had earned some money. Well, maybe he had not actually earned it, since I had done everything for him. But still . . .

This money business was a funny business. I was not sure I understood it. And Nancy and Bobby and I had not figured out the ten dollars they owed Mommy, either.

I sighed.

Then I sat up. I looked for my toy list. I read it over. Maybe it was time I had some fun with my money. Maybe it was time to buy some things for myself. I dumped out the money in my bank. I did not bother to count it, but I stuffed some of it in my wallet, and put the rest back in the bank. I made a decision. The next time Mommy drove downtown, I was going to pay a visit to the toy store.

I got my chance the very next day. When Mommy said she needed to go to the hardware store, I said, "Please can we go to the toy store after that? I want to spend some of my money."

"Well — " Mommy started to say.

"I will spend it wisely. I made out a list and everything."

"All right," agreed Mommy.

That afternoon I was standing in the toy store. My wallet was in one hand, and the list was in the other. I looked at the list.

"Bubble blaster," I said. I walked around the store until I found the outdoor summertime toys, and there were the bubble blasters. They are very wonderful bubble makers. I picked one up.

Next on the list were the pink slippers with white fuzzy trim for dress-up. I decided I better ask for help finding them. But the woman behind the counter said, "I am sorry. We do not have any pink slippers. Only silver ones. They are right over there." She pointed.

The silver slippers turned out to be a little expensive, but I picked up a pair anyway. Then I went looking for markers. What a selection. I could choose from an entire wall of markers. I took down the biggest package. (My arms were getting full.)

"Honey," said Mommy, "are you certain you want those markers? What about this package? It costs only about half as much."

I scrunched up my nose. "No, I like these." I dumped my things into a basket. Then I checked my list.

"Glow-in-the-dark bugs," I murmured. I found a box of them and tossed it in my basket. I tossed in a box of glow-in-the-dark dinosaur bones, too.

Next on the list was "something for Andrew." I called to my brother. "Andrew, I am going to buy something for you now. What do you want?"

"Could I have my own bubble blaster?" he asked.

"Sure," I replied. I added another one to the basket.

The last two things were stickers and art supplies. They were in the back of the store where I had found the markers. I began to load up the basket — glitter, paints, a needlework kit, a large box of crayons, and some glitter markers.

I was picking out stickers when I heard Mommy say, "Karen! My goodness! Look at your basket! Do you have enough money for all that?"

"I — " I started to say. Uh-oh. What if I did not? My basket *was* pretty full. I picked out one last sticker. Then I carried my basket to the counter.

"Karen," said Mommy, "now is your chance to put some things back if you do not want to spend so much money."

But I did not need to put anything back. I had enough money to pay for everything. I even had fifteen cents left over.

# B & N Gardeners

One morning I looked outside and saw a sign in Nancy's yard. I could not read it, so I ran next door. I stood in front of the sign. It said:

Home of B&N Gardeners
weeding and watering
call Nancy or Bobby

Underneath Nancy and Bobby's names were their phone numbers.

I was about to ring Nancy's bell so I could ask her about the sign, when I heard her say, "Hi, Karen! What do you think?"

Nancy and Bobby were lugging some things out of Nancy's garage — a pail, a watering can, and some gardening tools.

"It's a great sign," I replied. "What's B & N Gardeners?"

"It's us," said Bobby. "Bobby and Nancy Gardeners. We have finally started our business. We are going to ask the neighbors if they need us to do any gardening for them. Especially watering or weeding."

"We are very good at dandelions," added Nancy.

"That's a great business!" I exclaimed. It really was. Nancy and Bobby were smart. Everyone in our neighborhood has gardens. And they need plenty of help with them in the summertime.

"Thanks," said Nancy. "Well, we better get going. Where is Andrew?"

"Andrew? Why are you looking for Andrew?" I asked.

"He is our assistant," replied Bobby. "He is going to help us, and we will pay him part of the money we earn."

"Really?" I said.

"Yup," answered my friends.

Just then Andrew ran out of the house. "Here I am! I'm ready!"

"Andrew, what do you know about gardening?" I asked.

Andrew shrugged. "Nothing. I will do whatever Bobby and Nancy tell me to do."

At first I was not sure how I felt about this. My friends had started B & N Gardeners. They had asked my brother to help them. But they had not asked *me*. And I was Nancy's *best* friend. Still, I knew they just wanted to earn money for Funland. If they did not earn any, they wouldn't have much fun. And *I* wouldn't have fun if *they* were not having fun.

I followed B & N Gardeners to their first stop. I wanted to see if someone would give them a huge job. Maybe they would only need one huge job, and then they could quit and we could play together.

At the first house, Mr. Drucker asked B & N Gardeners to pull the weeds out of the cracks in his front walk. He paid them two dollars. Nancy got seventy-five cents, Bobby got seventy-five cents, and Andrew got fifty cents for being a good helper and always having the bucket ready.

At the second house they were paid fifty cents to water a garden.

At the third house they worked for two hours pulling dandelions, but they only earned four dollars.

"Boy," said Nancy, "this is hard work. And so far I have only earned two dollars and eighty cents." She wiped her forehead.

I felt a little sorry for my friends. They were all sweaty and dirty, and I did not need to earn a single penny. "You guys," I said, "come over to my house. I think I have some work for you."

"Really?" said Bobby.

"Sure," I replied. "Come on over."

We stood in my front yard. I looked around. "Well," I said, "I am sure Mommy would like those dandelions to be pulled up."

"More dandelions," muttered Andrew.

"And that new rosebush should be watered. And so should those flowers."

My friends set to work. When they finished, Nancy asked, "Who is going to pay us?"

"I am," I replied. I ran inside.

# Broke

I opened my piggy bank and dumped the money on the floor. I counted it out. One dollar, two dollars, three, four . . . nine. Nine-ten, nine-twenty . . . nine eighty-seven. "Nine eighty-seven!" I cried. Where was the rest of my money? What had happened to it? I thought for a moment. Well, I had taken my friends to the movies. I had treated everyone to Mr. Tastee's ice cream. I had given out lemonade money. And of course I had bought myself some things at the toy store. Somehow the money had just dwindled away.

I counted it again to be sure. Yup. Nine eighty-seven. That was all. And I owed B & N Gardeners two dollars and fifty cents. After I paid them I would have (I counted again) only seven thirty-seven for Funland.

Seven thirty-seven. That was no more than the other kids had. It was probably *less* than some of them had.

I stood up. I just could not believe it. I had had one hundred dollars for Funland. I was going to buy every souvenir and play every game in sight. Now I did not even have ten dollars. And what did I have to show for all the money I had spent? Not much. Just a few toys. Boy. No fair. If only Mr. Beadle had not shown up. (I could think of a few more "if onlys," too.)

I snatched up the two-fifty. I ran outside. I slapped it into Bobby's hand. "There!" I cried. "There's your old money."

"Hey, Karen. What is wrong?" asked Nancy.

"I spent all my money!" I replied. "That is what is wrong. I spent it on *you* guys. I took you to the movies. I bought you popcorn. I bought everyone ice cream. I gave people quarters to buy lemonade from Andrew. And now I am almost broke. I only have seven dollars. And by the way, you two still owe Mommy ten dollars."

My friends and my brother just stared at me. Finally Bobby said, "Karen, we did not ask you to spend your money on us."

"Yeah, you *offered* to take Hannie and me to the movies," said Nancy.

"And you offered us the ice cream," said Bobby.

"And I did not want you to go around giving out quarters," said Andrew.

"Anyway," said Bobby, "if you were going to spend all that money on us, why didn't you just pay your mother back instead?"

"Because *I* gave *you* the money!"

"Oh, forget about the stupid ten dollars,"

said Nancy. "Karen, I thought you *wanted* to treat us to those things. Because we are your friends. I thought you spent the money because you like us."

"Well, I did! But I did not mean to spend so much of it."

I was standing on one side of our walk. My friends were standing on the other. We glared at each other.

"Karen?" said Andrew finally. "Did you spend your money wisely?"

"No! No, I did not."

"But Mommy — "

"I know what Mommy said. And I thought I was spending my money wisely. I thought doing nice things for other people was wise. I guess I was wrong."

"Are you mad, Karen?" asked Nancy.

"Yes!" I cried. "Of course I am mad!"

"Well, I am mad, too. You said some things that were not very nice."

"I don't care."

"Fine," replied Nancy. "Good-bye." She spun around and walked away.

"Double good-bye," said Bobby, and he walked away, too.

Only Andrew and I were left. We stomped into the house.

"Karen? Andrew? What is going on?" called Mommy.

"Karen is mean!" yelled Andrew.

"Karen, please come here," said Mommy.

I went to the living room. "I did not spend my money wisely," I announced.

Mommy sighed. "Let's talk about it."

# A Hundred Bottles
# of Pop

The day of our trip to Funland had finally arrived. In my wallet was nine dollars and eighty-one cents, not counting my lucky penny. I was not sure, by the way, that the lucky penny was really so lucky anymore. For one thing, Andrew had more money than I did — eleven dollars and fifty cents. He had earned it all himself. For another thing, Bobby and Nancy were still mad at me, and I was still mad at them. (I had apologized to Andrew, though.) But I was afraid to throw the lucky penny away.

Throwing it away might be *bad* luck. So it was still in my pocket.

I had thought I might have more than nine eighty-one for Funland. I had thought Mommy might say, "Poor Karen. Let me give you five dollars for the trip." But she had not. Instead she said, "I guess you learned some things about keeping track of what you spend your money on." And then she had said, "Well, the trip is not for several more days. You have time to earn some money. And you will get your allowance." That is how I wound up with nine eighty-one.

On the morning of Funland day, my big stepbrother Charlie drove Hannie over to the little house. Guess who else he drove over. Kristy. She was going to spend the day sitting for Danny Dawes, Nancy's baby brother.

"Okay, time for Funland!" called Seth. "Everybody in the car!"

Andrew and Hannie and I scurried into our car. Next door, Nancy and her parents were climbing into their car. (Kristy stood on their front steps holding Danny.) Across the street, Kathryn and Willie were getting ready to leave, too. The Gianellis were probably doing the same thing.

" 'Bye!" Hannie yelled to Nancy. "See you at Funland!" She closed her door. "Karen," she said, "are you and Nancy still mad at each other?"

"Yes," I replied.

"Okay. Then I want you to know that I am not mad at Nancy. And I am not mad at you. So I do not want to be part of your fight."

"That's all right. You do not have to be." I was wishing that our fight were over anyway. I did not want to be mad at Nancy at Funland.

Seth started the car and we were off. The trip was going to last about an hour. We decided to sing songs. The last song we chose was "A Hundred Bottles of Pop." We were singing it when Hannie suddenly cried, "Oh, I see it! I see it!"

She was pointing out her window. And suddenly I saw it, too. T. Rex. "The giant dinosaur!" I said. "There it is!"

"And there's the Ferris wheel!" exclaimed Andrew.

Seth drove to the Funland parking lot. He parked our car with our friends' cars, and then we walked to the entrance in a big group. The grown-ups paid the admission fees, and we got our hands stamped. Now we could go on any ride we wanted all day long as many times as we wanted.

We hurried inside. "What shall we do first?" asked Mr. Dawes.

"The Ferris wheel!" cried Andrew and Alicia.

But the rest of us kids wanted to ride on T. Rex. So we walked through Funland, heading for the dinosaur. We passed souvenir stands. We passed cotton candy stands. We passed the midway games. We passed Cap'n Billy's Pirate Ship and Wild Water Mountain and the Jet Plane and Rocket to the Moon. So many excellent rides. But we kept going until we reached T. Rex.

The entrance to T. Rex was a dinosaur's mouth. We climbed into cars shaped like dinosaur eggs, two or three in each row. Andrew and Alicia sat together and of course, the Three Musketeers sat together. We heard a deep rumble and suddenly our egg lurched forward, into the dinosaur's mouth, under his red flashing eyes. And then we were in pitch darkness, zooming around corners, with dinosaurs leaping out at us.

We screamed until the ride was over. When our egg finally burst into the daylight, I saw that I was holding Nancy's hand. We looked at each other and began to giggle. Our fight was over. After I apologized to Nancy, I would apologize to Bobby. Then I could really have fun at Funland.

# Mr. Beadle Again

"Nancy, I am so, so sorry," I said as the Three Musketeers climbed out of the dinosaur egg. "I did not want to be in a fight with you."

"I did not want to be in a fight either," said Nancy.

I looked around for Bobby. "Bobby!" I called. "Come here."

Bobby ran to us. "Wasn't that a cool ride?" he said.

"It was awesome," I replied. "Bobby, I want to tell you something. I want to say

I'm sorry about our fight. I was mad at myself because I spent all my money. But I blamed you and Nancy. That was not fair."

"Well, I am sorry, too," said Bobby.

"You are? For what?"

"For telling you to pay your mom back the ten dollars. That was not fair either."

"Yeah, I'm sorry," added Nancy.

"It *is* hard to know what to do about that," I said. "I mean, who owes who the money? Plus you know what? Mommy has not even *asked* for it."

"Well, I have been thinking about it," said Bobby. "I decided Nancy and I should pay your mom back, even if she did not ask for the money."

"Yeah, B & N Gardeners is doing pretty well," agreed Nancy. "We can earn the money after Funland. No problem."

I smiled at my friends. Then I said, "Boy, money sure is hard to understand, isn't it? Look at all the problems it caused."

"It is very complicated," said Nancy.

"But let's not worry about it now," said Hannie. "I am just glad you guys are friends again. Come on. Let's go on another ride."

We went on lots of rides that morning. The Ferris wheel was next. After that, we could not agree on the third ride, so Mommy and Mrs. Dawes took the Three Musketeers until lunchtime. *We* could always decide what we wanted to do together. After our fourth ride, we decided to play some midway games, since we all wanted to win a stuffed animal. We played very carefully, since we were paying for the games ourselves.

By lunchtime, we had not won anything except rubber snakes, but we were having fun scaring each other with them.

"Girls! Come on!" called Mrs. Dawes. "Time to meet the others."

We had agreed to meet up with everybody for lunch. We met back at T. Rex, since the dinosaur is so easy to see. Then we tried to figure out where to go for lunch. This was not easy.

"No hot dogs," said Kathryn's father.

"Something healthy," said Mrs. Gianelli.

"I want ice cream," said Andrew.

I sat on a bench. I looked around Funland. I was thinking about which souvenir to buy when I saw someone who looked familiar.

The man smiled at me. "Karen Brewer?" he said.

"Mr. Beadle?" I replied.

"Yes! Well, how wonderful to see you. Please come meet my family." Mr. Beadle pointed to some tables at a refreshment stand. I saw a woman (she must be Mrs. Beadle, I thought), and a whole bunch of children. I counted them. Seven. Seven kids.

"This is our vacation," Mr. Beadle said proudly, after he had introduced me to his family. "We've been saving for it forever. Today Funland, and tomorrow the beach.

That is why I was so happy you returned my money."

*This* was Mr. Beadle's big vacation? Boy. It was just a day at an amusement park. I had been to New York City for a weekend, and I had flown out west to visit my grandparents, and in August my little-house family was going to the beach for two weeks. Whoa. I began to feel bad about wanting all of Mr. Beadle's money. I even felt bad about taking the reward. I could not return it now. But I was glad I had run into Mr. Beadle.

# 20

# Lost and Found

I was tired. It was late in the afternoon. We had been at Funland for hours. And we had had a blast. But now my legs were beginning to ache. And I was hot from running around in the sun all day.

Hannie and Nancy and I took a rest on a bench while the other kids rode on a water ride for the third time. Andrew and Alicia were sitting together, of course. We had liked the ride, too, but we were tired of drying off after it. (I think Mommy and Mrs. Dawes were glad we were tired. They were resting on the bench next to us. They had taken their shoes off.)

"I cannot believe you saw Mr. Beadle," said Nancy.

"I know," I replied. "I am so happy I did. And embarrassed."

"Why are you embarrassed?" asked Hannie.

"Because I had kept hoping Mr. Beadle would not turn up and I could keep his money. All I wanted was that eight hundred dollars so I could buy toys and Funland souvenirs. But Mr. Beadle really *needed* his money. He hardly has any. And he has *seven* children. And this is their vacation. Can you believe it? Boy, was I greedy. I wish I could give him back the one hundred dollars. But I can't. Anyway, I do not know where he lives."

"Karen? How much money do you have left?" asked Nancy.

"About two dollars. Why?"

"Let's all go buy a souvenir. I see a stand over there." Nancy was pointing. "And we have not bought souvenirs yet. Do you have enough money, Hannie?"

"I think so."

Mommy and Mrs. Dawes let us go to the stand by ourselves. They said they could watch us from their bench. Hannie and Nancy and I stood there forever, deciding. Some of the souvenirs were too expensive. But we could buy Funland sunglasses, or Funland visors, or Funland crazy straws. I really liked the red beanie hats with *Funland* stitched across the front.

We looked and looked and looked. Somewhere behind me I heard people bustling around, and voices saying, "Where is it? Where is it?" But I did not pay much attention. I had finally decided to buy the beanie. And Hannie and Nancy had finally decided on the sunglasses. I was reaching for my wallet when I looked down. Lying on the ground not too far away was . . . another wallet. No, this could not be happening.

I grabbed for it. Oh, please, oh, please,

oh, please. Let it be stuffed with money, I thought. And no name inside.

I opened the wallet. The first thing I saw was a card with a name on it: Seth Engle. Seth Engle? This was *Seth's* wallet?

I turned around. I saw the people and the commotion behind me. There were Mommy and Seth and Andrew and Bobby and everyone else who had come to Funland with us. And they were all looking for something.

"Where could it be?" Mommy was saying to Seth. "How could you have lost your wallet? You just had it."

I began to laugh. I ran to Seth. "I found it! I found your wallet!" I cried. "It was lying right here on the ground."

"Oh, thank goodness," said Seth. "It must have fallen out of my pocket after that last ride." Then Seth began to laugh, too.

It was time to go home. Hannie and Nancy and I bought our souvenirs. Then we headed back to the parking lot. As we walked through Funland, I said to my friends, "You know what? We spent an awful lot of money here today. And the only thing I have to show for it is my hat. And the rubber snake. But I still had a good time. I spent the rest of my money playing games and buying cotton candy. That was fun. I should not have been so upset about how I spent my one hundred dollars. You do not have to buy *things* when you spend your money. Having a good time is important, too. Maybe I did not spend my money the way I had planned, but I think I spent it pretty well, after all."

I rubbed the lucky penny. It was still in my pocket. I decided I might leave it there for awhile.

## About the Author

ANN M. MARTIN lives in New York City and loves animals, especially cats. She has two cats of her own, Mouse and Rosie.

Other books by Ann M. Martin that you might enjoy are *Stage Fright*; *Me and Katie (the Pest)*; and the books in *The Baby-sitters Club* series.

Ann likes ice cream and *I Love Lucy*. And she has her own little sister, whose name is Jane.

## Little Sister

Don't miss #51

KAREN'S BIG TOP

"Every circus member is a member of the B. F. Willie family. For the month of July, that includes every one of you."

Wow! His family was bigger than mine!

I hoped I would get to talk to his grand-daughter, Jillian. She was eight. I had a lot of questions to ask her about life in a traveling circus.

"And now the grand tour," said Mr. Willie.

He led us into a big circus tent and showed us all the equipment. The trapeze. The trampoline. The clown car.

"Can you believe it," I said. "We are in the middle of a real live circus."

# BABY-SITTERS™
## Little Sister
### by Ann M. Martin
### author of The Baby-sitters Club®

*More Titles...* ➡

------------------------------------------------------------

### Available wherever you buy books, or use this order form.

Scholastic Inc., P.O. Box 7502, Jefferson City, MO 65102

Please send me the books I have checked above. I am enclosing $_____ (please add $2.00 to cover shipping and handling). Send check or money order – no cash or C.O.Ds please.

Name_____Birthdate_____

Address_____

City_____State/Zip_____

Please allow four to six weeks for delivery. Offer good in U.S.A. only. Sorry, mail orders are not available to residents to Canada. Prices subject to change.                    BSLS497